The Longer the Wait, the Bigger the Hug

For Nana and Granny
E.M.

For Grandma Mary and Grandad Jim
P.D.

First published in the UK in 2021
First published in the US in 2021
by Faber and Faber Limited,
Bloomsbury House,
74–77 Great Russell Street,
London WC1B 3DA

Text © Eoin McLaughlin, 2021
Illustrations © Polly Dunbar, 2021
Design by Faber

Printed in Europe

PB ISBN 978–0–571–37040–5
HB ISBN 978–0–571–37038–2

The moral rights of Eoin McLaughlin and Polly Dunbar have been asserted

A CIP record for this book is available from the British Library

10 9 8 7 6 5 4 3 2 1

Laughlin  Polly Dunbar

The Longer the Wait, the Bigger the Hug

faber

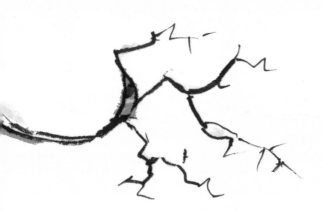

All winter Hedgehog
dreamed of Tortoise.

Winter was long
without a best friend.

Without a hug.

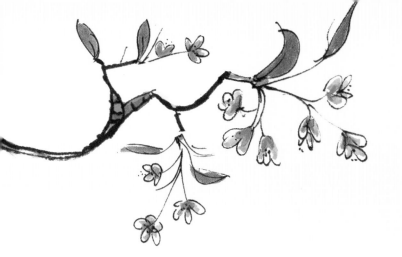

But when the sun tickled Hedgehog's
ears and spring finally arrived ...

Tortoise was nowhere to be found.

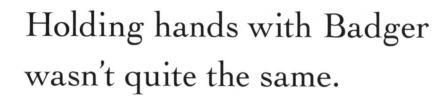

Holding hands with Badger
wasn't quite the same.

"It's jam."

The beach wasn't as much fun with Magpie.

Oof!

"Just ten more, please."

Hedgehog loved Squirrel,
but she wasn't very good
at hide-and-seek.

Hedgehog searched everywhere.
No stone was left unturned.
(Except for the heavy ones.)

But it was no good.

"I just want Tortoise."

Peep!

"The longer the wait,
the bigger the hug,"
said Owl.

"But I can't wait
any longer!"
said Hedgehog.

"Oh dear," said Tortoise.
"I must have overslept.

I was dreaming of you.

And the biggest, longest, huggiest hug...

EVER."

Faber has published children's books since 1929. T. S. Eliot's *Old Possum's Book of Practical Cats* and Ted Hughes' *The Iron Man* were amongst the first. Our catalogue at the time said that 'it is by reading such books that children learn the difference between the shoddy and the genuine'. We still believe in the power of reading to transform children's lives. All our books are chosen with the express intention of growing a love of reading, a thirst for knowledge and to cultivate empathy. We pride ourselves on responsible editing. Last but not least, we believe in kind and inclusive books in which all children feel represented and important.